The Wampum Exchange

❧

Rosemary McKinley

Cover Art: Rosemary McKinley
Copyright: © 2011 Rosemary McKinley
All rights reserved.
ISBN13: 978-0615724768
ISBN10: 0615724760

Acknowledgements

᭟

I would like to thank a few people who have helped me find the research I needed for this project. Melissa Andruski, archivist, and Dan McCarthy, assistant archivist at the Whitaker Collection at Southold Free Library delved into their collections to find any pertinent articles that I needed.

It wasn't an easy task, as not much was written about the daily life here in Southold in 1650. Melissa brought me to see a small, scale replica of the Barnabas Horton home at the Southold Pine Neck Museum Barn, which served as a model for the description of the home in the story.

I also visited the Old House at the Cutchogue Museum, the oldest Englisht type house in New York State. In addition, Dan also helped me in finding facts about agricultural life from this era in the Southold Historical Museum collection.

I spent some time at the Southold Indian Museum, researching how people at Fort Corchaug lived. Ellen Barcel was most helpful in pointing the way to continue my research. I used the displays of wampum found there to help me understand what it looked like and what it was used for.

I met with Jim Grathwohl to discuss the history of the area. He is also quite knowledgeable about both the history of Fort Corchaug and the English settlers who lived there. He directed me to study the research of Ralph S. Solecki, an anthropological expert on the fort. All of this information helped me to understand more about the daily life of the people and to write a story that was historically factual.

I truly appreciate the support and design work offered by my son, Peter. It was invaluable. I also want to thank Carl Jon Christensen for freely offering his computer expertise when I needed it. A special thank you goes to R. Jeffreys, 'Jeff', my editor, for working with me on the editing process. It was a smooth process because of the mutual respect afforded to me.

Dedication

Laura and Sam Giordano

Author's Note

᪥

When I moved into this area a few years ago, I was amazed at the rich history of the place. While researching information for my first book, I discovered that it was the first English settlement in New York State. Life in America, in 1650, was very different from what it is today. In the area known as Southold, which the native people called Yennicott, the land was filled with wildlife.

Wild game such as rabbits, deer, geese, turkeys and pheasants could all be found within the dense, virgin forests. Pristine bays and creeks were teeming with all manner of sea life and shell fish. There were few, roughened roads, so most people navigated by meandering trails that were cleared from the deep brush and woodlands.

Travel from farm to farm, and to the Meeting House (house of worship), which was the center of life for the early settlers could be difficult, especially during the colder months. The community was both the seat of government, as well as the center of religious worship. Each family was an integral part of these early settlements and each family had one vote in how they would all be governed. That honor was held by one male, per household. Each family in the community received a parcel of land that they farmed and where they produced almost everything they needed to survive in early America.

The Native people were here in America several thousand years before the Dutch and English settlers. Fort Corchaug, called The Great Place, by the native people was a wampum producing settlement. Part of it had a log stockade built for protection from the Pequots, and other warring tribes.

Today it has the only stockade known to exist of the eight known Indian stockades from the 1600's on Long Island. Most of their waking time was spent hunting, fishing, farming, and working with shells for wampum. They only went to the fortressed area when were under attack.

All of the research I found pointed to the fact that the native people and the settlers got along amicably, in the early years of the Southold settlement. I wanted to show this in my story, as well as the details of their daily life.

◈ ONE ◈

Spring

Daniel's first encounter with the Indian boy

Daniel raced down the trail. He ran towards the area where he knew geese were nesting. His dark, blond hair blew back in the wind, and reflected the sunlight, which streamed in and out of the tall, oak branches. The sun's bright rays blinded him for a few seconds, making him blink as he trotted his way through the deep woods. He needed to reach a particular spot to take aim with his long rifle; catching the geese resting and feeding on the ground, without scaring them away. The hunting spot was miles from his farm, so he had to move as quickly as possible to be home before dark.

There were no roads, only barely cleared trails connecting one farm with another. As Daniel navigated the trail, the sun momentarily blinded him again and he dipped his head down to avert the glare. He never saw the other boy, or the collision about to happen, until they ran straight into one another.

Whack!

The young bodies smacked together, with a noise that sounded like two, thick logs knocking together. They fell into a tangle of arms and legs onto the ground, and then quickly rolled away from each other. Startled and dazed, both boys laid on the ground for another minute, while they stared at one another.

Daniel could see that the boy was about his age but he was dressed very differently in tanned deerskin, with a bird's feather in his hair. The boy's eyes were a dark, charcoal color, and his straight hair was very long and black as a raven's wing.

Daniel was dressed in a coarse, tan colored, linen shirt and breeches that his mother had sewn for him. His eyes were as deep blue as a robin's egg. His hair was clipped at the shoulders and the color of beach sand.

Daniel had been told that an Indian tribe lived nearby but had never seen one before. Now, a native boy met his gaze right there in front of him. Both boys stood and examined themselves to see if they were hurt. They never averted their eyes from the other for more than a moment. Without speaking a word, both boys slowly turned and began walking in opposite directions.

Watching the native boy's back vanish into the trail, Daniel then noticed something peculiar lying on the side of the trail. He moved closer to better examine it, and found a necklace of some sort, made of white and dark blue shells. Daniel picked it up, and absently placed it into the right pocket of his breeches. He glanced once more to where the boy departed and then headed for home.

Earlier that day, Daniel planned to take time off to be by himself. He always had to ask permission but if he finished his chores to his mother's satisfaction, his wish was usually granted. Daniel liked the feeling of being independent when he went off to hunt. No one told him what to do. He could make his own decisions and be his own man.

Daniel said, "Mama, I'm going hunting. Be back later."

Martha watched her twelve-year-old son take the flintlock rifle off the wall over the mantle of the fireplace. He nimbly tucked the rifle under his left arm, while slinging the leather strap of the powder horn over his shoulder, as he walked out the door.

Martha was very proud of her son; his father had taught him well. They were good, honest, hardworking farm people. Her husband, Jonathan spent many days in the fields tending to the corn along with Daniel. Today, she knew Daniel was looking forward to going hunting by himself. She felt a greater sense of pride in the fact that he was now mature enough to hunt on his own. They were always in need of meat, especially when the colder seasons set in.

As Martha looked around her home, she methodically tucked her long, dark brown hair beneath her linen cap. Her hair continually fell down when busy with food preparation, mending clothing, or any of the other numerous, household chores she had to do. Her mornings began at sunrise, when she milked their cows and didn't end until all that day's work was completed.

Their house consisted of one, large room that served as a kitchen, dining, and living area all in one. There was a loft with a ladder, leading up to the sleeping area.

Martha fed her family a breakfast of Johnny-cakes—a type of corn pancake, and sitting on the table was a wooden pestle and mortar used to pound dried corn into flour. Martha was already preparing for the next meal of the day, and went down into the root cellar for carrots and squash stored from last fall's harvest.

She put the vegetables into a wooden dish and took them outside to wash in a large bucket of water that her young daughter, Clara, had filled from a nearby stream. Next, Martha stoked the fire under a big black pot that hung in the hearth they used for cooking meals. She swept up the twigs from the floor with a grass broom she' d made, and threw the twigs into the fire.

The hearth was made of stones the family gathered with great labor from the surrounding fields. Its rock chimney reached high up to the ceiling. Over the hearth was a thick, wooden mantle that had been hewn by Jonathan from a large tree. Plates and cups were neatly placed there. A powder horn and the family, flintlock rifle were set on hooks above the mantle.

On the stone floor of the hearth sat a large, cast iron grate that kept loose logs in place for the fire burning all year round, not only for cooking but to keep the house heated in the winter. The wood coals had to be constantly tended to by Martha and Clara. A black iron kettle filled with water hung just above the fire and was also used for cooking meals.

To the left of the main hearth was a rectangular, recessed area used as an oven for baking bread and pies. On the wall next to the oven hung a long, metal ladle used to stir the food, and iron tongs used to turn the logs in the hearth.

The main room was sparsely furnished and held their few belongings. In the center of the room there was a long, wooden table with benches on either side. Against one wall, a butter churner stood always at the ready. A spinning wheel was placed in the corner of the room to be used for spinning flax into thread. This thread would then be woven into linen cloth for clothing. Martha and Clara made most everything the family had to wear.

Their home was located in a clearing. Each family had help from their neighbors, as it took much time and labor to clear the land of trees, rocks, and brush. Surrounding the homes were thick forests. The sun filtered through the trees and allowed some light into the clearing. This time of year, the sun warmed the house as it rose in the sky. The sound of birds chirping in the morning reassured the family that spring was finally here.

Martha and Clara spent many hours tending to a kitchen garden set near the house. They grew carrots, radishes, beans, and peas in the spring and then cabbage, turnips, squash, and pumpkins in the summer and fall. There were always lots of chores to do on the farm to make sure there was enough food for the family, especially during the bitterly, cold winter months when fresh game was scarce.

The children were expected to help tend to the vegetables by weeding the garden, tilling the soil, and harvesting. Martha supervised the garden work and gave specific tasks to her children.

"Daniel, you are in charge of the weeding and hoeing today."

"Clara, you are to help Daniel with hoeing straight rows. The seeds and shoots need to be planted evenly, so we can yield the most food from our garden. I will check on you both, while supper is cooking."

Ten-year-old Clara had long, brown hair like her mother but the deep blue eyes of her father. She was especially fond of flowers. Whenever she saw them blooming, she cut some and brought them back home to her mother. Often, a pitcher of wildflowers was placed in the middle of the table, spilling over in all their colorful finery. Clara was always happy to be on the lookout for flowers and Martha always complimented her on her choices of blooms.

"Flowers brighten our house with their colors and scents," Martha often said to her daughter, with a smile.

Daniel approached the area where he knew geese were nesting and waited patiently. If he missed hitting his mark, the geese would scatter. It could take hours for them to return. Daniel had learned how to sit very still, while keeping quiet, before he set his spot.

While patiently waiting, he watched the calm, blue water of a nearby pond. The water rippled with small, white capped waves each time a goose touched down. When the timing was just right, he shot one of the geese. He picked up the now stilled bird, and started walking back home. He had taken this path many times before but was not aware that it bordered an Indian settlement.

About halfway from home, Daniel saw a man wearing a Dutch-styled hat. He wondered why the man was crouching down near to the ground. Although curious about the man's strange behavior, he didn't stop to ask questions.

Swiftly making his way home, Daniel hung his kill upside down on a hook attached to the side of the house to allow the blood to drain. Then he brought dried logs into the house and added them to the pile near the hearth.

Martha stirred a big pot of stew for dinner with a ladle. She asked Clara to prepare more corn flour for the morning meal by removing kernels from the husks and pounding them into flour.

"Daniel, wash up for dinner. Papa will be home soon. Then I want you to take out the Bible and find the passage I marked on Moses," Mama said.

Clara set the table with heavy plates and spoons. She then placed a tall pitcher filled with fresh cow's milk on the table. Clara listened while Daniel read the beginning of the story of Moses. The family Bible was never far from the dining table. Each child read passages from it daily. They had learned the alphabet at an early age as well.

After a while, Papa came into the house. Martha always smiled when Jonathan entered their home; watching him duck so he would not hit his head on the top of the doorway. Jonathan was a tall, strong man. He greeted his children and his wife, as they all sat down at the table to begin their meal.

"Daniel, say grace," said Papa.

"Lord, we thank you for our bountiful food, Amen," Daniel solemnly prayed.

They all began to eat and talk about their day.

"I see that you shot a goose. Where did you find him?" asked Papa.

"I went down to the trail by the bay," answered Daniel.

"There's an Indian settlement to the west, but it is quite a ways away," Papa said.

"Yes, sir, I heard that. But I've never seen it before."

"Some of the other families have met the Indians there. They don't speak our language but they are a welcoming people. They taught us how to plant corn, and even gave us some seeds to start our own crop. We have used their planting method ever since," Jonathan said.

Daniel then recalled colliding with the boy but decided not to say anything about the encounter to his father. He remembered the necklace he had in his pocket but didn't reveal that either.

After dinner the children were expected to get ready for bed. Daniel wore the shirt he had on as a nightshirt. Clara removed her blouse and skirt and wore her shift as a nightgown. The only light came from candles, so the room was dimly lit. Their parents talked awhile about their day, about how the weather was getting warmer, and that the corn and wheat were going to be planted on schedule.

Everyone turned in early because there were always so many chores to do in the morning. The chickens had to be fed, cows to be milked, and this all had to be done before sunup in order to get all the other tasks for the day done.

Papa tended the fields and Mama prepared food each day, while cultivating the garden. In addition, she spun yarn for cloth, made soap and candles, and worked hard keeping up with a multitude of other chores. Clara was now old enough to learn how to help with these chores.

✳

The next morning, as Daniel sat at breakfast, he absently placed a hand in his right pocket. He rolled his fingers around the necklace. Excusing himself from the table, he quickly walked outside to look at it more closely, so that no one else would see. The shells formed a pretty pattern. It was like nothing he had ever seen, yet he did not know what he would do with it. Mama did not wear any jewelry, and certainly not shells.

What should I do? He thought.

He had been taught by his parents not to keep something that didn't belong to him. How would he return it? Hastily, he put the necklace back into his pocket. In the back of his mind, he knew he wanted to meet that boy again.

But where do I find that Indian boy?

Shrugging his lean shoulders, he whispered to himself, "If I return the necklace by myself, no one will ever know that I had kept what was not mine to keep."

Today he was supposed to practice reading the marked passages from the Bible aloud to his mother. He went back inside and began reading. He came upon the Ten Commandments and as he read the words, *Thou shall not steal*, he kept seeing the necklace in his mind. Daniel was now quite perplexed about what to do.

"Mama, what if you found something that was not yours and kept it, would that be stealing?"

"Daniel, you know that a good person always returns something that belongs to someone else. Why do you ask?"

"I was just thinking about that while I was reading the commandments," Daniel replied.

In the late afternoon, Daniel went to meet his father in the fields. Jonathan was hard at work cutting some long branches that were to be used later for setting up a haystack.

Daniel called out to his father, "Papa, supper is ready!"

Both the man and boy headed home together. Supper was to be a sumptuous stew Mama prepared from some of the goose meat Daniel shot. She had added beans and turnips, and used wild onions and garlic as seasoning.

"Something smells really good in here," said Papa, with a broad smile as he bent low to enter through the door.

"Good job, Daniel. This is a real treat you've brought home for us." Papa winked, and patted him on the shoulder.

They were all looking forward to eating a dinner that included meat. Usually, their meals were mostly made up of the vegetables they grew and stored. Father and son washed up outside, while the table was set. Then everyone sat down to supper and held hands, while Papa said grace.

◦§ TWO §◦

Fort Corchaug

The Great Place of the Native Americans

The Indian settlement was home to about ninety native people. The summer wigwams served as shelter from the sun in the warmer weather. Dried cattails provided a thick thatch covering for the tops. A hole was cut in the top of the structure to allow smoke to escape from the inside. The wigwams were round and large enough to house a family of six.

Settlements were always set near forests and water, so the people would have easier access to what they needed. The bay provided ample fish and shellfish for many meals. Bark from cedar trees was used to provide many essential goods for the people.

Within the eastern part of the settlement, many women sat washing white, whelk shells and then placed them on the ground to dry in the sun. When dried these would be cut into fairly uniform shapes and small holes would be poked near the tops. This was done so that they could be threaded in rows over braided, rawhide strips. The shells, or wampum, would be fashioned into bracelets and necklaces to wear, and also exchanged as gifts for special occasions. The wampum shells were also woven into leather bands that the Indian people used to tell stories to the younger members of the tribe. The Europeans used the wampum to trade for furs.

Ambusco, the Indian boy who collided with Daniel, returned to the settlement after gathering acorns, still not realizing he had lost the necklace. His attention was instead focused on looking for his mother, wanting to find out when the evening meal would be ready. He found her near the fire pit, which was dug directly outside of their wigwam. She diligently washed the clams he had gathered earlier in the day. Next to the basket of clams was another basket filled with wild garlic and onions. These she used as seasoning for their meals.

Ambusco hungrily watched his mother prepare the meal. After she had shucked clams, she laid them on stones close to the fire, and sprinkled dried herbs on them for flavoring. Surrounding their wigwam were two poles hung with dried fish and one pole of dried deer meat.

She motioned to Ambusco that the meal was ready and to come and eat. Smiling broadly, with his stomach rumbling, he walked over and sat crosslegged next to her on the ground. She moved the clams from the hot stones with another large shell to cooler stones, so they could be picked up and eaten.

After he had eaten his fill, Ambusco reached for the pouch holding the acorns he gathered for his mother. Then he realized the wampum necklace was missing.

It was always placed on the top of the pouch to keep it closed, and now it was gone. He quickly decided to say nothing to his mother, and thought it would be better if he retraced his steps tomorrow and found the necklace.

Interrupting his thoughts about the missing necklace, his mother said, "Your father is still out hunting. He may be back with the next setting sun. Help me braid the cedar bark into twine. We will need it to make more necklaces to give him on his return."

He spent a few hours making twine with his mother, and then Ambusco grew tired and went off to sleep in his wigwam.

The next day, he planned on gathering more clams on the shore by the bay for his mother. His main purpose though was to find the lost wampum.

Where could it be?

He retraced his steps but still could not find the

necklace. He took his time looking on the sides of the trails, as well as in the grasses he walked through but the necklace wasn't found.

What would he tell his mother? The necklace did not belong to him; it was a part of the valuable wampum made by his people.

He did not know what else to do, except continue to look for the missing piece.

∽ THREE ∾

Summer

Baking days

Daniel awoke each morning to the sounds of his sister doing her chores. Clara brought fresh eggs into the kitchen each morning, along with a pail of fresh milk from their cow. His first task of the day was to make sure the hearth fire was burning hot enough for Mama to cook the morning meal.

Both Clara and Martha got up before the sun to feed the chickens and milk the cows. They always put on aprons before they set out to do their chores. This was to keep their clothes underneath clean.

After the early chores were done, Clara took out corn flour and set it on the breakfast table, as Mama heated the griddle for the Johnnycakes. Clara poured fresh milk into cups for the family to have with their breakfast. Mama fried up the Johnnycakes and everyone ate breakfast, while they talked and planned the day's activities.

Daniel usually went off to the fields and worked alongside his father. But today was baking day. One day a week was reserved for baking day; a day Clara looked forward to. Mama let her help prepare the dough mix for the bread. Once

Clara had proven to her that she could adequately perform this task, she let Clara knead the dough, as well.

Early in the morning on this day, Daniel was expected to monitor the fire by keeping it stoked, so the bread would bake evenly. He cut wood with an ax after he had dragged the larger branches home, to keep the wood box full. Other times, Papa would cut down dead trees near the house to replenish the wood pile as needed. The oven wood coals were kept hot, above and below the bread.

Mama removed the bread with a wooden peel— a flat wooden board attached to a long handle. All delighted in the aroma of the baking bread and couldn't wait to sample some. Since Clara was learning to bake bread, she was given the first piece to eat.

"Thank you, Mama, it's so good!"

"You earned it, Clara," said Martha with a bright smile.

"Clara, now please go down to the root cellar and bring me some onions, squash, and corn. I am going to cook some pork with them for dinner tonight."

✳

Clara went down into the root cellar and she saw the apples that were packed around straw in baskets. She was tempted to take one but decided to wait to ask Mama, first. As she passed one wall of the cellar, she brushed up against the dried garlic hanging in bunches from the ceiling and enjoyed the rich, deep smell it produced.

∽ FOUR ∾

Fall

Soap making, oh that smell!

Fall was the season for harvesting squash and pounding the dried summer corn into flour. Daniel and Clara spent part of everyday helping with these tasks. They did not mind them, however, no one in the family looked forward to the annual making of soap; it was time consuming and smelled awful. Martha chose a day that all four would be on hand to help. It was usually done in the fall, after butchering a hog, so that more fat would be available as an ingredient.

Jonathan's strength was needed at this time, since the kettle was extremely heavy to move. Daniel was expected to keep the fire burning under the cauldron. The entire process took a few days, but the soap they produced was enough to keep the family stocked for the entire year.

Mama said, "We will be making soap tomorrow. Papa and I need your help, so remember what we have to do."

Daniel and Clara replied in unison, "Yes, Mama."

Daniel piled wood ash from the fireplace in one

33

spot outside all year long near the house to be ready when needed. Martha saved the waste fats from cooking and butchering in a covered barrel. When Martha was ready to make soap, Jonathan dug a fire pit just for the special occasion.

Mama boiled water and placed a large basket over a barrel that had a small hole in the bottom. Then she poured boiling water over the ash, which then formed into lye. This dripped out of the bottom and into another container. The children were not allowed to go near the lye, as it could cause severe burns.

This process took several hours and when Martha thought it was close to the right consistency, she floated an egg in the lye. If it floated mostly above the liquid, then it was ready. This was then set out and left to cool.

The next task was to render the fat, which meant to remove the impurities. Soap needed pure fat for a more pleasant smell. Mama added equal parts of water and fat, and then boiled the mixture for several hours to melt the fat. This was the smelliest part of the process and had to be done outside.

"Clara, stand over here with me for a while," said Daniel, while holding his nose.

"Every year, this is the part we hate the most," Clara said laughing.

The odor was so pungent at that point everyone held their noses. Papa took the kettle off the heat, and more water and equal parts of fat were added. This was left to cool overnight. The fats would solidify and float to the top, forming clean fat, while the impurities settled to the bottom.

The last step in the soap making process was to use a kettle to boil the lye solution and the purified fat together, for about six to eight hours. When it cooled, it produced a purified, soft soap that had the color and consistency of brown jelly. The soap was then stored in a large barrel. The family used that soap sparingly, because they knew it had to last throughout the coming year.

After this tedious and smelly task was finally completed, Mama remarked, "This was a good year for soap because it was so much easier with all of you helping."

Once the kettle cooled, it had to be scrubbed to remove the smelly waste fats. It was brought down to the stream to complete the messy job.

Everyone would all agree and say, "Good thing this comes around only once a year."

Daniel and Clara always felt like they were a big help during this task, but they did not look forward to it, since the odor seemed to linger in the air for days after.

⤐ FIVE ⤏

Winter

Daniel's conscience sets him searching

When no one was around to see him, Daniel often took the shell necklace from his pocket and examined it carefully. Every time he did, he thought of the boy on the path. He knew he should return the necklace because it wasn't his to keep, yet how was he going to manage that? On his trips out to the fields, Daniel walked closer and closer to the area where Fort Corchaug was situated.

Somehow, he never seemed to get close enough to actually see it. Was he avoiding going there? What would he say to the boy? Daniel knew deep down that he must find a way to return what wasn't his.

"One of these days I have to see him again," he said. "I am afraid to tell Papa that I kept this necklace. I know he would want me to return it. Maybe I should tell Papa and then he can go with me to help find the boy."

One sunny day, on his way to meet his father, Daniel decided to side track to where he thought the Indian settlement was. He moved as quickly as he could. As he made his way closer to the fort, Daniel kept listening for voices of other people. He only heard the sounds of wind rustling through the branches and birds.

Then through a small clearing in the trees, he saw what looked like a fort. The people there wore deer hides as clothing and their shelters were built very differently from his own home. But he thought they looked somewhat like houses. He stayed back and observed, and what he saw amazed him.

There were many structures that he later learned were called wigwams placed near to each other. There was a walled area close to a grove of trees that was made from hewn logs. This embankment looked as if it was used for protecting the native people. One section, set far away from the living area, was filled with a large mound of white shells, and a smaller pile of blue ones lay next to it.

Women sat on the ground working on shells near the pile. From what Daniel could see, they seemed to be clipping the shells to a particular size. Others punched small holes into the shells. He saw that a few women polished the shells by rubbing them on a large stone. All of the people had long, black straight hair and dark eyes.

Daniel glanced around the settlement, looking for the boy he had met but he did not see him anywhere around.

He may be out hunting for food like I am, Daniel thought. Over to one end of the settlement was what appeared to be a plowed field. It was hard to tell because the cornstalks were cut down but he could see remnants of the plants and a few pumpkins and squash lying on the ground. Realizing that it was now getting late and he had to meet his father, Daniel was determined to return to the fort again. He would continue to search for the boy in hope of eventually finding him and returning the necklace to its rightful owner.

~ SIX ~

Late Spring

Working the land

"Remember where we planted the flax seeds?" Jonathan asked Daniel.

Yes." Daniel nodded.

"Now we have to harvest the plants and bring them to Mama. You will help Mama and Clara separate the fibers from the stalks. It takes a lot of time to do this chore. She needs the fibers, so she can clean and spin them into yarn. The yarn will then be woven into cloth, so Mama can sew new clothes for us to wear.

After we are finished harvesting, we will plow the fields. We will need old Bessie to carry the flax stalks back to the house and to pull the plow when we till the soil."

Daniel liked to help his father but every year the plowing seemed to get more and more difficult. Jonathan stood behind Bessie hooked up to the wooden plow. Every time the plow got stuck, Daniel ran ahead to remove a root, or move a heavy stone out of the way. Daniel liked working with his Papa but did not relish the hard work.

"Daniel, after we are done with the plowing, you

can go hunting for a few days. You will have earned it."

"Thanks, Papa." Daniel beamed at his father.

Daniel labored with his father for several more days working the soil. Both came back home dirty and tired.

"You were a big help this year, Daniel. You are getting stronger every day," Jonathan said proudly.

"Yes, Papa, I guess I am getting to be a man," Daniel said with pride in his voice.

"One day, Son, you will be but it takes more than hard work to become a man."

✳

Daniel had been given permission to go hunting, and he was free to wander the forests and trails for a while. Each time he went hunting, he edged closer to the Indian settlement. Often, he just stood and watched the older people hard at work and the youngest children at play. He thought he might find an excuse to enter the settlement but he did not have the nerve to go alone.

✳

"I will begin the planting tomorrow Daniel. I need your help."

"Yes, Papa. I know."

"After breakfast we will take Bessie and the cart to carry the wheat and rye seeds to the fields. You're big enough to hold the reins now." Papa smiled.

Daniel jumped up from the table and was excited. "Really, you will let me do that?"

"Yes, Son, it is now your time."

The next morning, father and son filled the cart with the seed bags. Daniel carefully steered Bessie to the fields. They sowed the wheat and rye seeds on one side of the field, and then planted the corn, beans, and squash seeds on the other side.

"Plant the corn seeds in the middle, Daniel. Later, we will sow the bean seeds, so they will grow up around them. After a few weeks we will plant the squash seeds in a larger circle around the beans. We learned this way of planting from the people at the fort, when we first came here."

Daniel was always amazed when the seeds began to sprout. The stalks got taller and the vegetables grew bigger as the weeks and months wore on.

↬ SEVEN ↫

Early Summer

Haystack making

There were always numerous chores to do on the farm. One of the major chores was to build a new haystack each year. Papa chose to place the haystack between the house and the field, so Bessie, their ox, could eat her breakfast close to the house.

Every May, Papa began stacking the branches and orchard grasses for the haystack, which provided enough food for Bessie for the year. Daniel was expected to be on hand to help him, as the work required two people. Papa cut the grasses in the early morning with a scythe, after the dew had dried somewhat. This task took most of the morning to complete. After the harvesting they spread the tall, cut grasses out to dry in the sun.

"Daniel, you should keep brushing the grass off your shirt. You look like a scarecrow!" Papa laughed loudly.

"Yes, Papa," Daniel replied, with a grin of his own.

At high noon the work stopped for dinner. The hard work made them both hungry. Mama had wrapped Johnnycakes in cloth for them to eat.

They sat in the shade, while enjoying their meal.

When it came time to build the haystack, Papa dug a hole and placed a tall branch in the ground, a few feet deep to secure it. They took smaller logs and placed them in a crisscross pattern, around the bottom of the pole. Then they took some of the longer grasses and twisted them into a long rope. Papa wound the rope around the tall pole to seal the hay close to the inside of the pole.

They continued piling grass up to the pole and around it to form a beehive shape. The grasses had to be tightly packed or rain and wind would crumble the haystack. This allowed the outer grasses to stay stiff and kept the inside hay dry. Although the job took many hours with the two of them working, it was a necessary one. Bessie had to have hay to eat each day.

"You have been a big help, Son. Two people working together makes all the chores easier," Jonathan said, while gently clapping Daniel on the back.

"Thank you, Papa. I see that we can get twice as much work done, in the same amount of time as it takes one person to do the same chore. I am learning that the more hands you have to help, the easier it is to finish the work. There sure are a lot of chores aren't there, Papa."

"Yes, Son. There are."

❧ EIGHT ❧

Summer

Clara's Lessons

Every morning Clara helped her mother with the chores. At first, it was not easy to learn how to milk their cows but Mama was patient and Clara managed to learn. Now, every morning Clara milked the cows and fed the chickens. Her job was to ensure the family would have milk for the delicious Johnnycakes Mama cooked on the griddle. Even the chickens looked for her and seemed happy to see her because they knew she was going to feed them.

Every Saturday, Clara had another hard chore to do. She had to dump the picked beans onto a large basket and separate them from the rocks and twigs mixed in amongst them. Mama simmered the cleaned beans in a large cast iron pot of water with onions, salt pork, and molasses. The meal was set on the stove each Saturday night and left to simmer slowly for supper on Sunday after church services.

"There is no work on Sunday. You cannot do any chores except the absolutely necessary ones," Papa said.

After Sunday breakfast, Daniel hitched Bessie

to the wagon and they would go to the meeting house for several hours. Clara liked the quiet day but did not enjoy standing so still for such a long time, while listening to Reverend Youngs' sermon.

On week days, Clara practiced spinning flax into thread on the spinning wheel. This was a very tedious and time consuming task to do. Once she had added enough threads to the pile, Mama weaved them into cloth. When Mama had enough material gathered, she sewed shirts and breeches for Papa and Daniel, and a shift for herself. When she had small squares of cloth left over, she made mob caps (bowlshaped caps) for Clara.

She made Clara a pinafore, which is a short apron to keep the underclothes clean when she milked the cow. Mama sewed the everyday clothes with extra care and she made special clothes for Sunday services.

Martha often commented, "Clara, you and Daniel are growing like weeds. I feel like I'm sewing new clothes for both of you every week!"

Each day after chores, Clara took out the Bible and read from a passage that Mama had set with a scrap of cloth. She learned her alphabet at a very early age, so she could read the passages without too much trouble. Mama listened to Clara read while she weaved and helped her when she stumbled over a particular word.

"I want to be a good person but sometimes it is not easy to do. Especially, when I want to go off and look at the colorful birds flying overhead, instead," Clara mused.

She loved being with Mama but she longed to sit for a while and play with her doll.

Mama saved scraps of linen so they could dye the fabric to make new dolls for Clara. They used cranberries found floating in the marshes for coloring the cloth. For hours they let the linen soak in the juice from the squeezed cranberries, and then let the cloth dry by the fire.

With Mama's help, Clara carefully stitched squares of white linen placed over the top of a twig for the doll's face. For the doll's body and lower legs, she used a thick twig with a v-shape and turned it upside down to form legs. She then wrapped the dyed cloth around the twig many times to form a body. Next, she took some charcoal from the fireplace and drew eyes, a nose, and a mouth for the face. She even had some white material for a tiny hat. When finished, the doll was dressed like a little version of Clara, who held the doll tight whenever she felt lonely or afraid.

One day, when Mama opened a trunk upstairs to remove their Sabbath clothes, Clara saw a baby's christening dress. She asked if she could use the dress for her doll. But Martha told her that this was too precious to use for play. She said she was saving the rosebud, embroidered gown for another baby.

"Someday, when you marry, Clara, you may want to use this for your own baby, my dearest."

"Yes, Mama, I never thought of that." Clara smiled shyly at her mother.

❧ NINE ❧

Sabbath

The one day of rest

Sundays were always welcomed because they were the only days of rest. Every other day of the week everyone in the family had chores to do to keep them all fed and clothed. Sundays were different. Families could not do any extra work; it was part of their religious beliefs.

"Morning Mama," said Clara sleepily.

"Morning Clara," replied Martha. "Hurry child and feed the chickens. I'll milk the cow this morning. As you know, we are not to do any work that is not necessary on the Sabbath."

"Yes, Ma'am, I know."

Mama and Clara headed out to do the chores. They returned to the house with milk and a few eggs. After breakfast, they washed and dressed in their Sabbath clothes. These were always clean and ready for such an occasion as going to services. Mama took them out of the wooden trunk that was stored up in the home's loft. Their shoes and woolen capes were brought here from England, before the children were born. Everyday clothes were not always clean, because they wore them all of the other days, and they did get sweaty and dirty sometimes.

When it was warm, the children bathed in the stream near the house, while Martha washed the clothes and placed them on a tree branch to dry. Everything dried quickly, because it was warm. Mama washed their clothes less often in the winter, because these would not dry as quickly hanging by the fire hearth.

Papa and Daniel hitched Bessie up to the wagon so they could all travel together to Sunday services.

Mama said, "Jonathan, I remember when all of the men in these parts gave their time and helped build the Meeting House. It has served us well. I heard that there is a public meeting next week about some land question. Yes, all of our hard work paid off. Each family has a house and land to grow our food. The cleared land is needed to add a few more families to the area. Here we are, every Sunday, listening to Reverend Youngs reminding us of what God wants us to do."

The Meeting House was a large building, built with finely hewn logs and had wooden shutters to cover the window openings. All of the community members were there to listen to Reverend John Youngs preach.

Most of the men attending services had built

the meeting house. It was used for all public town meetings, as well as services. In the winter it was always cold inside, and most of the families stood, but some sat on benches, huddling to keep warm.

The cemetery was located on God's acre next to this very important building. It was called that because the people believed that the cemetery and house of worship should be close together.

It was hard for the children to stay awake for such a long time and to stand for so long.

Yet, they looked forward to services. Because, after listening to the preacher for many hours and saying prayers, they got to visit with other members of the community and play with the other children. Usually the adults gathered in a group and talked about their week, amongst themselves.

Reverend Youngs prepared a sermon each week, to help the congregation think about the almighty Father. The last few weeks he had been talking about each of the Ten Commandments. This particular week he was talking about the sin of stealing.

"Members, the Lord does not want us to take what is not ours. Stealing is a grave sin, even if we do not mean to take something from others. If we steal an ox, a cow or a chicken, we are openly taking food from our neighbors' mouths. We all know that is wrong and against God's law, but what if we find something that another has lost? Is that a sin? What if we did not intentionally take another's property? Is it still a sin?"

Reverend Youngs paused, as he stared intently at his congregation and then continued speaking again, with an increased fervor in his voice. "The unmistakable answer to all present here is yes, indeed, I tell you! You must always do the right thing and return anything that is not rightfully yours. If things are gotten in an under-handed way, cast them out. Return them to their rightful owner!"

The reverend's sermon went on for over an hour, but Daniel only heard this particular part of it. And, it struck him hard. His stomach turned into knots and he felt nauseous. Did the Reverend know about the necklace? I am in trouble, Daniel frantically thought. What am I going to do? He told himself to keep calm. He had to find the courage to tell Papa.

"I must tell Papa about the necklace," he whispered. Daniel had finally made up his mind.

After services, the family went to stand before two, small graves to pray. Mama and Papa's two baby daughters were buried there.

They died in childbirth, their parents told them.

Mama wiped her eyes after a prayer was said. The markers said Prudence and Penelope but no one talked about them much. There were many other tiny graves in the cemetery. Many other families had also lost their babies.

By the time the family returned home, it was time for a meal. The beans had been cooking all day and were ready to eat. They said grace and had their meal. After a long day of attending services and meeting with other families, everyone was hungry.

Mama added bread to their dishes, so there was enough to eat. After supper, when they had relaxed for a while, they read passages from the Bible and talked about their meanings. When the discussions were over, the children sat and played quietly, as there were no chores to be done on the Sabbath.

When they were at the last service, the men reminded each other about a meeting that they were all expected to attend on land sales. Papa mentioned this to Daniel after dinner.

"On Thursday next, I want you to come with me to the meeting, Daniel. It is time that you learned how these meetings work because they are important to our community. Besides, some day you will be allowed to vote. You know that every man has one vote."

"Yes, Papa," said Daniel, feeling more grownup than ever before.

⍋ TEN ⍋

Fort Corchaug

The Indian ways

On a clear day, when Daniel was out hunting again, he found himself once more near Fort Corchaug. It seemed to call to him. He continued to search for the boy he had run into months ago. He kept far enough away so no one at the settlement would see him but close enough so he could observe them.

In utter amazement, this time he recognized the boy. He heard the others call him Ambusco.

Aha, he thought, with a satisfied feeling. At least, now I know his name.

Ambusco appeared to be about the same height as Daniel. He wore what looked like a deerskin apron around his waist, with no shirt.

Daniel noticed that everyone seemed to have a task to do, except for the youngest children. As he was about to move closer to the settlement, he saw all the children join together in a group, and then sit in a circle.

One of the Indian women walked into the center of the circle of children, and began to speak.

Daniel could not understand the words but all the children remained quiet and seemed mesmerized by what she said with both her hands and voice. The woman waved her arms and Daniel believed this was part of the way she told the story. She reminded him of the way Reverend Youngs preached to the congregation. Daniel now listened as intently as the children in the circle, while the native woman spoke and gestured.

✦ ELEVEN ✦

The Indian Woman's Story

The Magic Footprints

"Once, long ago there was a Corchaug Chief so tall and so swift, that when he leaped, he jumped from one far shore to the other."

The native woman jumped from one spot to the next, to show this part of the story. The children's eyes grew bigger, as she stretched her arms out to illustrate a great distance.

"One print of his foot was left behind on Orient Point. Another was left on a big rock on Shelter Island. The third and last one landed right in the middle of our fort."

The woman pointed to the spot where they were sitting, and all the children seated around the circle gasped.

"They must have been magical footprints because the story goes that they fit the feet of all who found them, though they might be as big as a giant, or as small as the smallest child."

The woman pointed toward her moccasin clad feet and the children stared wide-eyed.

✳

Even though Daniel could not understand the language, he was mesmerized by the way the woman acted out the story. When she finished her tale, the children left the circle and went back to their play.

Daniel turned his attention back to a cultivated field. He saw many women tilling the soil with hoes made of large shells. He could see many circles of stalks of corn in the middle, with squash growing around the corn, and beans winding up the stalks, just like his father told him they had learned from these people.

✤ TWELVE ✤

The Meeting House

Daniel's first meeting with the men

After an early dinner, Papa and Daniel readied to go to Thursday meeting. Daniel felt very proud to be included.

Papa said, "Daniel this is a meeting about land and I want you to attend. You will learn our ways, and how things are done in the town."

"Yes, Papa, I will listen and learn," Daniel replied.

When they arrived at the Meeting House, almost all the men from the other families were there.

Calling the meeting to order, Mr. William Wells said in a loud voice, "Here Ye! Here Ye! We have spoken to the leader at Fort Corchaug about purchasing more land. This particular acreage needs much less clearing, as it is on a broad plain. What do all of you think about this plan?"

The men discussed this important issue for half an hour, and after this matter was addressed, Mr. Terry brought up another issue. The leader at Fort Corchaug had told him, through an interpreter, that a man had stolen a large cache of corn the past fall. They wanted to know if anyone here had seen a stranger near the fort. Some men replied that they had seen a man they thought was a Dutchman by his clothing, although they were not sure.

Mr. Terry said, "The people at the fort are not happy about this thievery, as they would gladly have shared their seeds with anyone who asked. Remember that is how we got our first corn seeds. One of the men from the fort gave us a bag of seeds years ago. He even showed us how to plant them. We need to investigate this urgent matter further."

All the men nodded in stern agreement.

Upon hearing Mr. Terry, Daniel had a sinking feeling in his stomach, as he remembered seeing a man near the fort last fall and had thought nothing of it at the time.

What should I do? Daniel thought, as he connected the event with the day he found the necklace. He said nothing at the meeting but decided he would talk with his father about it on the way home.

When the meeting ended, father and son returned home in their wagon. On the way back, Daniel began to cry. He couldn't hold back the tears streaming down his face. He could hardly speak but forced himself.

"Papa, I have to tell you something important."

Jonathan looked down at his son and could see the discomfort in his face. "What is it, Daniel?" Papa asked softly.

"The man they just spoke about at the meeting, the one who may have stolen the seeds."

"Yes, Daniel. What about him?"

"I was out hunting last fall and saw a man crouching down in the woods. It may have been him. I also ran into an Indian boy that same day and he dropped a necklace. I found it and kept it without telling you."

"Daniel, why haven't you told me about this?" Jonathan's voice was now demanding.

"I was afraid to tell you, Papa. I know I shouldn't have kept it but I thought I could return it by myself. And when I found where the fort was, I didn't want to go into there alone."

"Oh, Daniel. You should have told Mama or me," Papa sighed. "We would have found a way to settle this. Son, you know stealing is a sin."

"I know Papa, I was listening to Reverend Youngs' sermon," cried Daniel.

"I will talk to Mama when we return home and we'll find a solution to this problem together. Daniel, you know you should have told us when this first occurred."

"Yes, Papa, I know and I'm very sorry."

They were both silent for the rest of the trip. When they arrived home, Papa told Daniel to prepare for bed. Daniel did as he was told but was still upset by the conversation in the wagon. Daniel couldn't help but overhear his parents as they discussed the necklace.

"Now, we have to go to the elders and bring Daniel, so he can tell them what he saw. Daniel has to learn that keeping the necklace was wrong. It does not belong to him," Papa said.

"Yes, Jonathan," his mother replied with an even tone. "But I could see why he did not go to the fort alone. He should have come to us right away. That is his fault. He has to learn to do the right thing. These people have shared much with us and they deserve to be treated well."

Daniel tried to listen to the entire conversation, although he was afraid to hear what his punishment would be, but he was so tired he fell asleep.

The next morning, chores had to be done as usual. Clara continued doing her daily tasks and so did Daniel, who fearfully waited to hear what his parents had chosen for his punishment.

Unlike most mornings, he ate very little because he was so anxious about what his parents had decided. Jonathan let everyone quietly finish their breakfast, before he spoke to Daniel.

"Daniel, your Mama and I have decided what you will do. I will go with you to the fort and we will return the necklace to the boy together. You will not be able to go hunting again until we say you can. You will also help Mama and Clara with more of their chores during the day.

And Thursday next, we will go to the meeting and you will be called to give witness to the elders. You will tell them that you saw a man on that day, and you will tell them about the Indian boy's necklace you kept."

"Yes, Papa." Daniel looked at his lap, feeling ashamed.

Daniel was sad and afraid to do what Papa told him he must do but he knew he had to follow through. He had broken the commandment— *Thou shall not steal.*

The next week passed without much time for Daniel to think about the meeting. He was too busy helping his father in the field, his mother and Clara with churning milk into butter, and grinding corn into flour.

One person was still very curious about the whole story. Clara wanted to know everything. Why had Daniel not told her? When they were out of earshot from their parents, Clara eagerly pressed her brother for information.

"Daniel, let me see the necklace. What does it look like? Is it special?"

Daniel decided to show her the necklace, instead of answering all of Clara's many questions.

"Look, for yourself." Daniel placed the stringed shells in Clara's hands. "So what do you think? Is it worth anything? Is it special?"

Clara stared intently at the object. "I would say it is special, even though I have never seen anything like it, Daniel. Why didn't you tell Papa that you found it? He would have known what to do."

"I wanted to return it on my own but I was afraid to go alone," Daniel whispered.

"You know what this means, you will be whipped at the meeting house."

"Yes, I know. That is why I am afraid," cried Daniel.

Clara placed her hand gently on Daniel's shoulder but said nothing. She knew what was going to happen to Daniel and felt sorry for her brother. But she knew he had to be punished because it was their way.

๏ THIRTEEN ๏

Day Of Reckoning

Meeting night

As the next meeting approached, Daniel felt like a knot had grown in his stomach. He knew his father wanted him to do what was right and answer any questions truthfully. Daniel kept thinking of Ambusco and wondered if he had told about the missing necklace. On Thursday afternoon before the meeting, Jonathan arrived home and summoned his son.

"Daniel, I want you to honestly answer any questions the men at the meeting ask you this evening."

"Yes, Papa, I promise I will."

"You must tell exactly what you saw on the day you met the Indian boy. The elders will decide how we will return the necklace. They speak with the leader there and will know how to settle this."

"Papa, I am scared. I don't want to say the wrong thing," Daniel said, fear evident in his voice.

"As long as you tell the truth, you won't say the wrong thing. Besides, we have to find a way to return the necklace, and your testimony may solve the mystery as to who stole the corn seeds," his father said.

Daniel walked outside, hitched Bessie to the wagon and they headed off to the Thursday meeting. Daniel was unusually quiet and visibly nervous. When the meeting began, Mr. Wells called the elders to order and the upcoming land deal was once again discussed. All the men voted for the sale. It would add to their land holdings and this particular parcel was already cleared, so there would be less work for the community.

After the voting, the Reverend stood up to speak. Daniel thought that he would be preaching a section of the Bible but that was not the subject of his speech. Daniel was, and he now nervously stood next to his father and waited to be called.

"Daniel Horton has something of great importance to tell us tonight," Reverend Youngs stated.

Daniel walked to the front of room and faced the men. His voice quaked and cracked but he steadied himself and began to tell the story. Even though he knew he would be punished, he felt the burden of guilt falling from his slim shoulders. The longer he spoke the stronger his voice became.

"Last spring, I was running down a trail near Fort Corchaug and ran smack into an Indian boy. We both fell to the ground, and after we got up, he just went off in the direction he had come. We didn't speak. Then I saw something on the side of the trail and picked it up. It looked like a shell necklace.

"I never said anything to anyone about it because I thought I could return it by myself. But after a while I was afraid to walk into the fort alone. Now I know that I should have given it back. It is stealing, even if I did not take it on purpose. I am sorry that I sinned, and I will willingly take my punishment."

Daniel stood up straighter, as he looked around at the men's faces and then glanced toward his father.

He began speaking again and his voice was even stronger now. "Another strange thing happened that day. I saw a man I didn't recognize off to the side of the trail, near the fort. He was crouched down and it appeared that he was looking for something. He wore a Dutchman's hat. He didn't notice that I was watching and I did not say a word to him."

Reverend Youngs cleared his throat and said to Daniel, "Thank you for your witness, young man. Yes, Daniel, you should have told your father of these matters right away, and not waited until now to tell us here. We will decide your punishment but first you must return what does not belong to you.

"Secondly, you may have helped to solve a

crime, since the leader of Fort Corchaug reported someone stole seeds around the same time as these incidents occurred.

"I cannot guarantee this but these facts you've told us this evening may lessen your punishment."

The Reverend placed his hand on Jonathan's shoulder and said, "Mister William Wells will go with you and your father to the fort and clear up this matter, as soon as it can be arranged. I know this was not easy for you to do, Daniel. Thank you for your honesty and testimony tonight."

Reverend Youngs placed his other hand on Daniel's shoulder and smiled down at the boy.

Daniel stood silently and now felt relieved of the very heavy burden he had carried for a long time. He felt happy that he might have solved an important matter that affected the entire community, too. He watched Papa speak with Mr. Wells and Reverend Youngs, as they set the date to meet at the fort.

Back in the wagon, Daniel was silent again. He expected his father to now admonish him.

Instead, Jonathan said, "I am very proud of you son. You told the truth, even though you knew that punishment would be a consequence. I now know that you will always do what is best for the community, even if you are punished for it."

"Thank you, Papa. I understand now what you mean about becoming a man. It is much harder than I thought. Sometimes owning up to a bad choice is harder than anything else, but it means I am growing up, too."

"Yes, Daniel, you truly are." Jonathan put his arm around Daniel's shoulder and hugged him.

When they returned home, Daniel was so tired that he climbed up to the loft and fell into a sound sleep. The was the first deep sleep he had in many months without his conscience bothering him.

❧ FOURTEEN ❧

Lost And Found

The Wampum Exchange

The following week, Daniel and Jonathan met with Mr. Wells at the entrance to the fort. Daniel had never been on the inside and he tried to absorb everything at once.

This time he could clearly see each wigwam and the women moving in and out of them. He saw baskets of clams and fish close to each, as well as bowls of nuts. Off to one side women worked on shells from the big mound. Some used a tool to punch holes in them, while others rubbed shells on a stone to polish them.

Off to the other side, near the field, women collected squash and corn. Over by the stream young men caught fish with their hands, and others with sharpened sticks. It looked to Daniel that everyone here was busy at a task.

Mr. Wells brought Daniel and his father to a circle of men near the tallest wigwam. Mr. Wells was one of only two men in the community who had learned the basics of the Indian's complicated language of speech and hand gestures. He went to the leader, Mamoweta, and they spoke quietly with each other. They had developed a good relationship over the past few years, and it was clear they had mutual respect for one another.

Mr. Wells then brought Daniel to sit in front of the leader, just as Ambusco was summoned from a nearby wigwam. It seemed to Daniel that the boy and Mamoweta looked alike, and he wondered if the two were related. Daniel noticed that the boy had a bracelet of blue and white shells on his upper arm.

As soon as they saw each other, they smiled.

Daniel pointed to his chest and said, "Daniel."

Ambusco pointed to himself, and said, "Ambusco."

The Indian boy watched intently as Daniel took the necklace from his pocket. Ambusco looked puzzled but when Daniel handed it to him, the Indian boy smiled wider.

The leader took the necklace from Ambusco and examined it. Mr. Wells leaned over to the leader and they made some gestures towards the necklace and pointed out toward the field. Mr. Wells then pointed to Daniel and said something to the leader.

Mamoweta listened and nodded back.

Mr. Wells stood and said, "We are done here. Mamoweta now understands who most likely stole the corn and doesn't blame anyone in our community for the theft." Mr. Wells then turned to Daniel, "The leader is grateful to you, Daniel for returning the necklace to his grandson."

The leader spoke to Ambusco and then pointed to Daniel. The Indian boy approached and gripped Daniel's forearm with his right hand. Daniel realized that this act was a gesture of friendship. He gripped Ambusco's arm in the same way and both boys grinned at each other.

Now it was time to depart for home but Daniel would return with Ambusco's friendship in his heart.

As they walked toward the wagon, Mr. Wells asked, "Daniel, do you know anything about wampum or its value?"

"No, Mister Wells. I had never seen anything like it before the day I found the necklace," Daniel replied.

"The necklace you returned was more valuable than most because it had dark blue shells, as well as white ones. A necklace like this would be exchanged to mark a special occasion, and is held in the highest regard and honor. It was a good deed to return it for that and many other reasons. I believe that our friends at the fort appreciated it," Mr. Wells said with nod of approval.

On the way home, Daniel felt elated by his new friendship and that the necklace was now in its rightful home. But thoughts of what punishment from the elders might still befall him crept back into his mind.

"Papa, what will happen to me, now? What will my punishment be? I am still afraid to stand in front of the elders again," Daniel said, with tension returning to his voice.

"Daniel, you did the right and noble thing, even though it was not easy. Whatever your punishment is, I know you will take it like a man. You've grown so much in front of my eyes these past few days. You will come to the meeting with me again and we will face the elders together," declared Papa.

✎ FIFTEEN ✎

Daniel's Punishment and Promise

The boy becomes a man

The following Thursday, Reverend Youngs spoke at the meeting on many topics, including finalizing the land agreement. The last topic of discussion was left for Daniel's punishment.

Reverend Youngs turned his attention to Daniel and said, "Please stand, young man. We have discussed your punishment at length. You came forward and returned the necklace to the people at Fort Corchaug, and you helped to solve a crime, that helped to maintain peace between our community and the native people. Yet, you must be punished.

This is the law that every member of this community must abide by and honor. Without laws in place to protect all in the community, there would only be chaos and rampant crime. Your punishment is thus, your father will whip you five times with a switch."

Daniel's face drained of all color, while he stood and listened to the Reverend. He looked at the elders and his father and lowered his head.

The ride home was spent in silence and Daniel was glad to not have to speak again that evening.

His mother waited up to hear the decision the elders had made about her son. Martha nervously asked Jonathan what was to happen to Daniel. When Jonathan told her the punishment, she was sad for her son, but resigned to the fact that he must take it and learn from it.

The next morning, Jonathan told Daniel to go to a nearby tree stump. "Bend over, Daniel. Let us get this over with and move on with our day."

Daniel did as he was told and Papa hit him with the switch five times as directed. He closed his eyes and clenched his jaw until it was over and tried to think of something else.

In the meantime, Clara quietly ran to the corner of the house where she could not be seen and listended to the sound of the switch. She clung to her doll and prayed that Daniel would not be in too much pain.

Jonathan broke the switch over his knee and said, "Daniel you've learned many important lessons over the past few days and I am very proud of you. You are now the second man of this house."

"I am glad this is all over with too, Papa. And I know that I have learned many lessons I will not forget. I promise you."

Daniel now felt as if he had grown much closer to being a real man. The men at the Thursday meetings offered him their respect, too. Daniel was included in the meetings, although not the discussions, since he did not have a vote yet.

As Daniel grew older, he learned to communicate with the Corchaugs and acted as an interpreter, just as Mr. Wells had done before him.

Ambusco eventually became leader of the Corchaug tribe, and he and Daniel became life-long friends. His Indian friend never forgot the return of his precious necklace, and Daniel always remembered the important lessons he learned as a boy.

❧ END ❧

About The Author

❧

Rosemary McKinley began writing to both entertain and inspire others. Her book, 101 Glimpses of the North Fork and Islands was released in 2009, and led to interviews by radio station KJOY and the Suffolk Times.

Her short stories, essays, and poems have been published online by the Visiting Nurse Association of Long Island and in Lucidity, LI Sounds, Clarity, canvasli.com, Peconic Bay Shopper, Fate Magazine, Examination Anthology, The Ultimate Teacher, and Newsday.

Made in the USA
Middletown, DE
11 September 2017